JUN 9. 93

AUG 2. 5?

MONSTER CRIMES UNIT

CONFIDENTIAL

FRANKENSTEIN'S MONSTER

LAPD

OCT 12. 84

RESTRICTED MATERIAL

DISCARDED

DEC 11. 77

MAR 22. 04

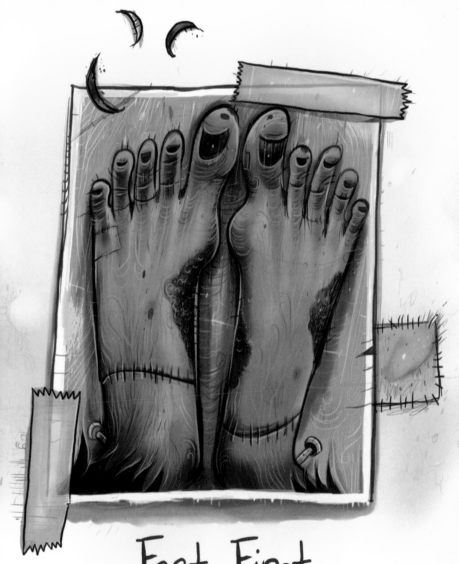

Feet First

BORRRRING. That's how I'd describe the first 13 years of my life. Don't get me wrong . . . living at Mr. Shelley's Orphanage for Lost and Neglected Children® wasn't ALWAYS bad. But, more often than not, life was just a big ol' heaping helping of boredom.

Thankfully, Year #14 made up for it all. Which is why I'm writing this journal. Because Year #14 needs to be remembered (or at least not forgotten).

So, in case you were wondering, my future self, here's what you looked like then . . .

In fact, the place was GOING OUT OF BUSINESS!

One day, Mr. Shelley got a letter. The power company said they'd be shutting off the power sometime in the next 24 hours.

And that's when this monster mystery started . . .

"That'll do it," said Mr. Shelley from inside his office. "I guess this is the last time I'll see this place. Or it would be, if I could see anything with the lights shut off!"

I went into his office and handed him a flashlight.

"Thank you, J.D.," said Mr. Shelley. "I really don't know what I'd do without you. But I suppose I am about to find out.

"I'm sorry I wasn't a better director, J.D.," he said, the corners of each eye sprouting a tear. "Sorry I couldn't find you a family. Sorry I failed at yet another business and can't repay my brother-in-law the money he loaned me to open this orphanage.

Sorry I have to move to Las Vegas and work in his ice cream truck to pay back what I owe."

Mr. Shelley shivered at the thought.

"Don't panic, sir," I told him. "I'll figure something out. I promise."

MR. SHELLEY

"You always say that," said Mr. Shelley. "And you always do it, too. Without you, this orphanage would have gone out of business a long time ago. I always said you were my right-hand man."

He had always said that. I had always thought that was weird, since my LEFT hand is way bigger and stronger than my RIGHT.

"You were the one keeping this place afloat," he continued. "I was just holding you back. It's probably better for you that we go our separate ways. But before we do . . ."

Mr. Shelley used the flashlight to find a box under his desk.

"The bank is going to repossess the building  and everything in it. We're only allowed to take our personal stuff. This is yours," Mr. Shelley said, putting the box on his desk. "This is the box I found you in outside the orphanage."

The only thing inside the box was a blanket.

"You were lying on that when I found you at the door," said Mr. Shelley proudly. "You never forget your first orphan. I remember it like it was yesterday."

I couldn't say I remembered that, but then, I was just a baby. I picked up the blanket to take a closer look. The blanket reeked of must and dust.

I let out a sneeze.

ACHOO

"Oh my!" exclaimed Mr. Shelley.

"It's no big deal," I shrugged. "Just my allergies."

But Mr. Shelley wasn't looking at me. He was gaping at the bottom of the box. Underneath where the blanket had been was a book.

"Well, what do you know about that!" exclaimed Mr. Shelley. "I never even thought to look under the blanket." Then he sighed. "Shows you what a bad orphanage director I was."

I opened the book. It was a journal (kind of like the one I'm writing in now). Only someone had already filled all the pages of this one. And as I flipped through them, a photograph fell out. It must have been stuck in between the pages. I picked it up.

It was a photo of a baby being held by . . .

FRANKENSTEIN'S MONSTER!

Not that there's anything strange about that. I had seen plenty of photos of Frankenstein's Monster.

A while ago, maybe ten years — or no, I think it was almost fifteen years ago — Frankenstein's Monster made a BIG SPLASH before disappearing without a trace. No one had seen or heard from him since.

From what I remembered reading about him, Frankenstein's Monster hadn't been a bad sort of monster. (Not like the Mummy — that guy left a big mess in the middle of town a couple years ago!)

On the back of the photo was a note:

One day, you'll know why I had to leave
forever. But I want you to have this so
you'll know where you came from.
Love, Dad

I looked at the baby again. Even though he couldn't have been more than a couple months old, I could see that one of the baby's legs was shorter than the other. His left hand was way bigger than his right. And he had one green eye and one blue one.

That baby was me! HOLY CRUD . . .

My dad was Frankenstein's MONSTER!

Chapter 2

WELL, THAT EXPLAINED A LOT!!

Like why one of my eyes was blue and the other bright green. Why one hand was huge with long fingers, the other small with short, stubby ones. Why both my feet were way too big for my legs.

They all came from different parts of different people that went into my father!!

It was a lot to take in all at once. For thirteen years, I never knew anything about my family.

And now . . .

It was kind of like discovering your dad was a king or a famous rock star. Only mine was a monSTAR!

But it gave me an idea.

I had always dreamed of having a big family. Sure, my dad was gone. And I didn't even know if I ever had a mom. But that didn't mean I didn't have a family out there. Parts from dozens of people went into my dad. All those people were a part of him, and he passed their hands, feet, eyes, and hands to me.

Which meant the people who went into him were kind of related to me. I figured those people were probably all dead. (At least, I hoped they had been dead before their legs, arms, and feet were taken from them to make my dad!) (GROSS!)

But those people whose parts went into my dad . . . they probably had relatives who were still alive. I was related to them too. They were my cousins!

Which meant, somewhere out there, the thing I'd spent years daydreaming about was actually true! I had a MONSTER family! A family made up of the descendants of the dozens of people whose parts made up Frankenstein's Monster.

All I had to do was track down where each part of my dad came from to find them!

I said all that to Mr. Shelley as we stood there in his office, looking at Dr. Frankenstein's journal with the flashlight.

The journal was hundreds of pages of notes, scribbles, drawings, and maps. It didn't have an index, or a glossary, or whatever else you call those parts of books that tell you where to find what you're looking for inside.

I had no idea where to start.

"How about at the beginning?" suggested Mr. Shelley, pointing to the cover.

DUH!

If found, please return to

Dr. Victor Von Frankenstein,

423 Greenbush Avenue

Chapter 3

First thing the next morning, Mr. Shelley dropped me off on his way to Las Vegas. He had been very relieved I had somewhere to go. Mr. Shelley's brother-in-law had insisted there was room in his ice cream truck for only one more, and Mr. Shelley didn't want to argue with him. I couldn't blame him. From what I had overheard of their phone conversations, his brother-in-law sounded pretty tough for an ice cream man.

I said goodbye and thanked Mr. Shelley for everything, including the ride.

Having lived my whole life in the same room at Mr. Shelley's Orphanage for Lost and Neglected Children®, I didn't have a lot of experience finding my way to new places.

After Mr. Shelley drove off, I forgot to breathe for a minute. What if this didn't work? What if I never found my family? What if they didn't want me to find them? What if they were happy without me? And how could an orphanage director leave a kid behind without even waiting to see what happened to me?

Actually, the answer to the last question was pretty obvious. Mr. Shelley never was a very good orphanage director.

"Don't panic," I told myself, like I'd told Mr. Shelley a thousand times. "I'll figure something out."

CREEPY!!

I double-checked the address to make sure I had it right. But I already knew I did. Every house on the block looked the same. Except this one.

19

This one looked like a HAUNTED CASTLE.

I knocked on the door. A minute later, a voice came from inside: "Yes?"

"Um . . . is this the Frankenstein residence?" I asked, hoping I didn't sound as nervous as I was.

"Yes," answered a muffled voice through the door.

Would Dr. Frankenstein be some kind of scary mad scientist with wild hair? Or a nice old man who wanted to help me?

As the door began to open, I tried to be ready for anyone or ANYTHING.

FRAN

I totally wasn't ready for what I finally saw.

Holding the door open was a GIRL, maybe three or four years older than me. "This better be important," she said. "You're interrupting a moment of brilliant insight."

← MY FIRST CRUSH!

"Oh," was all I could think to say.

I had been expecting some ancient scientist, not a teenage girl. It didn't help that she was kind of cute, too.

"Okay then," she said, starting to shut the door.

"Wait!" I said. "I'm here to see Dr. Frankenstein."

That got her to stop closing the door slowly.

Instead, she slammed it shut — **WHAM-O!!**

"No one by that name lives here!" she shouted through the thick door.

"But, but —" I pleaded. "You said this was the Frankenstein residence!"

She opened the door a crack.

"I must have misheard you," she said, looking down her nose. "This door is very thick. I thought you said the Fran Kenstein residence."

"Right," I nodded. "Frankenstein."

The name made her shudder. "No," she said, annoyed. "Fran Kenstein. My name is Frances Kenstein. There is no Frankenstein here!"

"Oh," was all I could think to say again.

I felt like someone had jumped on my stomach and pushed all the air out.

If this was a dead end, I didn't know where to look next.

"Are you ill?" she asked. "Something about you looks a little . . . off."

"Oh, no, that's just me," I said. "I get my looks from my dad," I added proudly.

"I must have made a mistake," I told her, picking up my bag to go. Although I had no idea where I'd go. "It's just, I found this journal, and it said —"

I reached into my bag, past my own journal, and pulled out Dr. Frankenstein's.

As soon as I did, her eyes lit up. Like there was a glittery flashlight inside each one.

They actually kind of sparkled. (Give me a break. I said she was cute, didn't I?)

"Why didn't you say so!" she exclaimed as she grabbed my big left hand and dragged me inside the house. "Come in!"

It was the **FIRST TIME** I had ever held hands with a girl.

Fran sat me down in her kitchen and offered me anything I wanted in her fridge. When I opened it, the only thing I saw inside was big ol' bowl of GUACAMOLE.

"Sorry if I was rude before," she said as she placed the bowl of green stuff in front of me. I was hungry, but I wasn't sure how to eat it. There didn't seem to be any chips.

"Dr. Frankenstein was my father," she told me. "But I'm so sick of hearing his name. I'm tired of people comparing me to him. I'm a brilliant scientist myself, you know. I was in the middle of a RIDICULOUSLY challenging experiment when you knocked on the front door."

"Oh," I said, impressed. She was cute AND smart!

"I want to be my own person and do great things of my own without people always thinking of Dr. Frankenstein when they hear my name," she said. "You can understand that, can't you?"

"Definitely," I nodded, because it seemed like the right thing to say. But actually I didn't really understand. Nobody had ever thought of my dad when they heard my name. Mostly because, until today, nobody — including me — knew who my dad even was.

"So that's why I changed my name," she said.

"To Fran Kenstein?" I asked.

"Exactly." She nodded as if that made perfect sense. She took a bite of guacamole. Which wasn't as easy as it sounds without any chips. Or even a spoon!

"I've lived alone in this house since my father died," she said, pointing at the kitchen and the large house beyond. "Doing my own experiments. Which are really quite brilliant.

"But enough about me." She smiled, and then gave me a serious look. "Let's talk about my father's journal! I had no idea where it went. Your dad must have stolen it. He and my father never really got along very well."

"Hey, wait a minute!" I said, then stopped short.

I was about to stick up for my dad. But then I thought, maybe he did steal Dr. Frankenstein's journal. I didn't know him well enough to be sure he wouldn't do something like that (he was a MONSTER, after all). And Fran seemed to be positive that he had.

Suddenly, I realized something else.

HMMMMMM...

"Wait, did you know my dad?" I asked excitedly. "What was he like? Did you know my mom? Do I even have a mom?"

I had a million more questions. But Fran stopped me before I could get any of them out.

"There's so much I can tell you," Fran said. "But first we should get to work on finding out who the people who went into your father were!"

I couldn't believe it. I hadn't even told her why I had come here, and she was going to help me do it!

Did I mention she was cute, too?

Fran asked if she could see her father's journal. I reached into my bag and pulled out a book.

"WHOOPS! That's my journal," I said, stuffing it back in my bag. "Here's your dad's."

Fran took it and started scanning the pages into her computer on the kitchen table.

"Once the pages are scanned, it will be easy to cross-reference and find whom each part of the monster came from," she explained.

I felt that happy tingling in the back of my shoulders I only felt when I was sure something AWESOME was about to happen. I loved that feeling.

True, every time I had felt it before, the awesome thing I was sure was about to happen turned out to be a HUGE DISAPPOINTMENT.

MAYBE.

But I was sure this time would be different.

"And as soon as I find where each part of the monster came from, I'll be able to build a new one," she went on. "And when I do, no one will ever compare me to my father again!"

"You mean, after you do the same thing he did?" I asked, confused. That didn't seem like the smartest idea to me. But I knew Fran was really smart. (Mostly because she kept telling me.)

"I've tried so many times to build my own monster," Fran explained. "I'm not going to say I failed, because a genius never fails. Those setbacks were a necessary part of the process. They showed me that there was something special about the parts that went into the original that made it work. I realized that to have any chance of recreating the monster, I would need to use the same genetic material. I could get that from the people whose body parts went into the original monster. If they were still alive. Bodies that have been dead for too long don't work anymore. My other experiments proved that."

DNA

For some reason, I didn't want to ask what those other experiments were. Yikes!

"But there's another possibility," she went on, scanning more pages from the journal. "I could use body parts that share the same DNA. The left arm from a relative of the original left arm. The right eye from a descendant of the monster's right eye. But the problem, of course, was finding those people.

"And then you show up!" She smiled. "With my father's journal! He was a maniac about writing things down. I'm sure that somewhere in his journal is all the information I need to track down every single living descendant of the people who went into his monster!

"Once I use them to create a new monster, no one will ever compare me to my father again!" she exclaimed.

"You mean, after you do the same thing he did?" I asked, still confused.

"Exactly!" she nodded, as if that explanation made perfect sense.

"But how are you going to do it?" I asked her. "I mean, I'm sure all those people are using their feet or eyes or whatever."

Fran just smiled a creepy little smile. And then I got it. Oh, no! No way!

She is crazy!

"Okay, wait. Hang on. You may be cute," I said, and then wished I hadn't. "But I just found out I have a family. I haven't even met them yet! I'm not going to let you use them for some kind of experiment!"

"It's not an experiment!" she roared. "I know it will work! Just like I know this will work . . ."

Fran pushed a button on the counter next to her. And then I, the stool I was sitting on, my journal, and the bowl of guacamole fell into darkness.

"WHOA!" I cried, falling down and out through an opening in the side of the house. **CLANG!** A metal flap slammed shut behind me as — **SQUOONCH!**— I landed in a pile of moldy guacamole. (GROSS!) My journal splashed down next to me.

I picked it up and put it in my bag. I was in a small pen with a doghouse.

Fran must have sent me down the shoot that she used to feed her dog!

Only what came out of the doghouse was no dog. Or maybe it had been once. The awful BEAST was clearly one of her experiments.

It growled hungrily. Then, the "dog" opened its mouth (at least, I think it was its mouth) and leaped!

But not at me — at the fresh guacamole. As it snarfed it down, I climbed onto the stool, balanced on my big feet, and jumped over the fence. I ran around the house and back inside through the open front door. But when I got to the kitchen door, I stopped short. What would Fran do to me when I came in?

I counted to three. And then four. And then FIVE. And then I charged into the kitchen! What I saw was even scarier than I had imagined. FRAN WAS GONE! And she had taken Dr. Frankenstein's journal with her!

Chapter 4

The house was empty. Fran could have been anywhere by now. Well, not anywhere. She was probably headed straight for my family! I had to warn them. Only I didn't know where — or even who — they were!

"Okay, don't panic," I told myself. "I'll figure something out."

I looked around. On the computer screen were the pages of Dr. Frankenstein's journal she had scanned in. I could see they talked about my dad and his parts. I started printing them out.

But which body part was Fran after? She could be tracking down any one of them.

I took a deep breath and thought it through. She had run out without closing the front door. She must have seen something that made her jump up and rush out. What could have made her do that?

I looked at the last thing she had scanned from the journal. It was a TOTALLY gross drawing of a pair of feet. When I looked at those feet, I didn't feel grossed out. Instead I was shocked.

Those teeny toenails! The bumpy ankles. The feet in the drawing looked just like MY feet!

But there was something else that made my hair stand on end: The words scribbled on the bottom of the page. "Subject: Mr. Percy of Victorville."

Mr. Percy must have been the man my dad got his feet from!

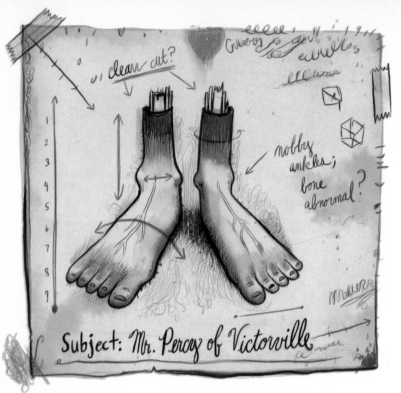

Subject: Mr. Percy of Victorville

I didn't even have to type the town or the man's name into Fran's computer. They were the last things in her search history. I clicked on the one article in the list that was highlighted in green, meaning it had already been read. It led to an article about Mr. Percy, a famous explorer who lived in a small town called Victorville.

That must have been the location where Fran was headed right now!

I had to get there before she did and warn him! Even though I had no idea where Victorville was or how to get there.

As I jumped up to rush out, I accidentally hit the mouse and clicked on another link. It brought up an article, which said that the famous explorer Mr. Percy of Victorville had died many years ago (I hoped before Dr. Frankenstein got his hands on his feet!).

I remembered what Fran had said: bodies that were dead for too long were no use to her. So I sat down and did a little more digging.

Turns out, Mr. Percy had a son. His name was Robert — and he was an explorer too.

I printed out the most recent article I could find about him. It talked about Robert's expedition to an island in the South Pacific.

According to the story, Robert didn't bring any of his high-tech exploring gear with him on this expedition. He had to use what he found. He lived on bananas and used coconuts to mark his trail. Blah, blah, blah. That didn't really interest me.

But the photo did . . .

"'I lived on bananas and used coconuts to mark the right way to go,' said the explorer Robert Percy."

In it, Robert was barefoot. He had the same teeny toenails and the same bumpy ankles as I did.

No doubt about it . . . he was my cousin!

The article mentioned that an Explorers Club had sponsored Robert's trip. That was a couple years ago. I couldn't find any more recent information on Robert, but a quick search revealed that the Explorers Club was right here in town.

Fran didn't know any of that — it wasn't in her search history.

Which meant while she was chasing a dead end (literally), I had a chance to find Robert before she did!

I took out my journal and wiped the last bits of guacamole off it. There were still plenty of blank pages in it, so I taped in all of the scanned pages I had from Dr. Frankenstein's journal, as well as the article about Robert.

Then I printed out a map of town with the Explorers Club marked on it. I taped that map to a page too.

That's when I realized: I had used Fran's computer to do all this! She could probably figure out how to retrieve my search, just like I had found her search!

Even if I tried to smash the computer or delete the search, someone as smart as Fran could probably figure out a way to retrieve it.

But there was no time to worry about that. I had to get to Robert first! Grabbing my journal, I rushed to the door.

And then I stopped.

I ran back to the refrigerator, grabbed all the guacamole, and dumped it down the leftovers chute. I didn't want the beast outside going hungry. I didn't know when Fran would come back. I just hoped that when she did, it was without my cousin.

Chapter 5

Outside Fran's house, I opened my journal to the page with the map taped to it. In all the time I'd lived at the orphanage, I hadn't done much exploring around town. But I had a map. How hard could it be to find the Explorers Club?

Somewhere about the time I stepped in the dog poop taking a shortcut through a park, I realized I must have made a mistake. And not by turning left when I should have turned right.

I mean, I must have made a mistake thinking I could be related to an explorer!

I was just about the opposite of an explorer. I couldn't find my way anywhere!

A couple hours later, my feet were sore all the way from their bumpy ankles to their teeny toenails. But I had found the Explorers Club.

The building looked like a cross between an Egyptian pyramid, the Great Wall of China, and an igloo. I figured every time one of the explorers got back from somewhere, they must've added something from that place to the building.

I pushed on the front door, which looked like it could have come from an Aztec temple.

CREEEAAK.

The door swung open.

Inside, the hallway was lined with huge paintings. A sign above them read "Past Members." One of the pictures showed an explorer being swallowed by quicksand. Another was of a man being mauled by a tiger in a jungle. The rest were even more gruesome.

HOPE HE'S OKAY!

At the end of the hallway, I heard voices coming from behind a door that looked kind of scary.

(It didn't smell all that great either.)

But there didn't seem to be anyone else in the whole building.

So I took a deep breath and pushed the door open.

Inside was a men's room, crowded with a dozen or so very old men.

"I say," one of them said to me, "you're a little peculiar looking for an explorer."

"Oh, no, I'm not an explorer," I replied. "The front door was unlocked, so I just . . ."

The old men nodded.

"Hmm . . . must have forgotten to lock that again," said one of them. "But then, we seem to be forgetting a lot of things these days. We were headed to the dining room just now when we forgot the way and ended up here. Rather embarrassing for a group of explorers, wouldn't you say?"

I didn't know anything about exploring or explorers, so I told them I really couldn't say.

"Anyway, it's nice to meet a young man with an interest in exploring," said a tall explorer.

"So tell us, where have you been?" said another. "Anyplace exotic? Nothing explorers love more than a good tale of a trip to the exotic!"

The other explorers nodded excitedly as they crowded around me.

"Well, besides Mr. Shelley's orphanage," I told them, "the only place I've been is here."

They all looked disappointed.

"To be honest," I said, "before this morning, I didn't even know that there were explorers anymore. Well, except Dora —"

BED HEAD!

All the explorers let out a groan.

"Sorry," I said, embarrassed. "I know that's just a cartoon."

"Oh, no, that show is based on a very real explorer," said the tall explorer. "Doratea Emma Maria is a member of this club. An excellent explorer. Just not as good of an explorer as I."

"Or I!" said another.

"Or I!" echoed the rest.

"You know, those television people actually approached me first," said the tall explorer. "They wanted to make a show about MY explorations. Only I couldn't remember them!"

"Doratea always did have a good memory," said another explorer. "That's her strong suit. That and her counting."

He turned to me. "Now then," he said. "What brings you here?"

I told him I was looking for the explorer named Robert Percy.

"Doesn't ring a bell," said the tall explorer. The other explorers murmured in agreement. My stomach sank.

"No, wait!" said the tall explorer. "Now I remember. Robert is a member of this club. But he's not here at the moment."

Holy crud! I found him!

I mean, sure, I had to wait for him to come back. But I had waited my whole life to find my family. I could wait a little longer.

"When will he be back?" I asked.

The tall explorer looked at me. "Well, my best guess would be . . . never."

Chapter 6

I stared at the tall explorer. I was sure I must have heard him wrong.

"Could you say that again?" I asked.

"Did you forget already?" He smiled. "Don't worry. Happens to me all the time. The explorer you're looking for is on a journey to the last unexplored part of Antarctica."

"An Antarctic explorer?" I sputtered, unable to think of anything else to say.

BRRRRR!

"Quite a mouthful, isn't it?" said the oldest explorer. "That's probably why there are so few."

"And now it seems there will be one less," the tall explorer said with a sigh.

"This is the last email we received from Robert," said the oldest explorer, taking a folded piece of paper from his jacket pocket. "Before all contact was lost with him. I can't remember how long ago."

"We keep forgetting to go after him," said the tall explorer. "Besides which, we are probably too old to do it anyway."

The others nodded sadly. Except the oldest explorer. He smiled and pointed at me.

"But you're not old!" he shouted. "You're the youngest explorer here! You could rescue him! Here, take the email. It might help you."

He shoved the email into my hands.

"But I'm not an explorer," I reminded them. "I don't even know where Antarctica is! How would I even get there?"

None of the explorers had an answer for that.

"I'm headed that way," said a voice.

Everyone turned. Standing there in the open door to the men's room was a woman who was probably thirty years old. Or maybe forty. (It's kind of hard to tell when people get that old.)

"Doratea!" exclaimed an explorer.

"In the men's room!" exclaimed another.

"Bah," scowled Doratea. "Is it not an explorer's duty to go where others think she cannot?"

All the explorers had no choice but to nod and mutter that she was right.

Doratea turned to me. She wore an old leather pilot's jacket over a purple shirt and orange pants.

A pair of flight goggles sat on top of her jet-black bangs.

"*Vamanos*," she told me. "Let's go!"

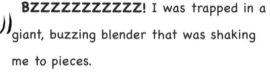

*   *   *

BZZZZZZZZZZZ! I was trapped in a giant, buzzing blender that was shaking me to pieces.

I woke up from that dream to find myself being rattled in my seat as it bounced in the small cockpit of Doratea's seaplane. The buzzing came from the engines, which felt like they were about to shudder the plane apart.

"You have slept for a while," said Doratea, her eyes fixed on the cockpit's window, or windshield, or whatever you call it. "We are nearly there. I hope we are not too late. Roberto has not communicated in over a week. He may not have very much time left.

"He is my boyfriend," she added in a worried voice.

"How do you know Roberto?" she asked.

"Oh, I don't know him at all," I replied. "But he's my cousin."

I told her my story. (I left out a couple of the embarrassing parts.) It took a while. It would have been easier to just let her read my journal, but her hands and eyes were busy flying the plane.

Doratea smiled grimly when I was finished. "I see," she said. "Well, it seems we both have very good reasons to want to rescue him. Luckily for us, I have this map!"

Doratea nodded at the map on the floor between us.

Her map! If it were anything like the map on her TV show, we'd definitely find my cousin!

"How does it talk?" I asked, grabbing the map and trying to find its mouth.

Doratea looked like I had just picked my nose and offered her a taste.

"It doesn't talk," she replied. "It is a map."

"Oh," I nodded, not wanting to risk saying anything else that would sound so dumb.

"But," she went on, "this map can still tell us many things. It's a copy of the map Roberto took with him on his expedition. Look."

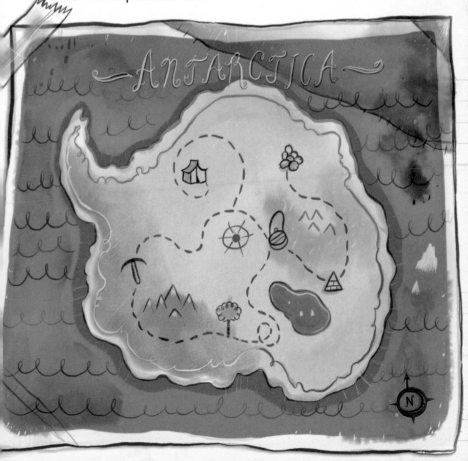

"What do these symbols mean?" I asked.

"I don't know," replied Doratea. "Those dotted lines must be different paths Roberto considered. But I do not know which one he took. That we will find out together after we land."

"We are *muy circa* — very close," said Doratea. "Look . . ."

I looked out the cockpit window. I knew I should have been impressed. But everything was just white.

"So this is Antarctica," I said, trying to sound excited.

"No," replied Doratea. "This is a cloud."

DUH!

She pushed down on the steering wheel or whatever you call the thing that drives a plane. As we nosed down, the engines rumbled louder and louder.

"This," shouted Doratea, "is Antarctica!"

YUMMMM!

Suddenly, there it was!

The snow was so bright in the sun it almost glowed. The whole thing looked like the top of a vanilla frosted cupcake.

It was the most beautiful continent I had ever seen.

As I stared down, I saw a ship, or a sloop, or whatever you call the kind of boat rich people own, sailing toward the shore. Doratea saw it too and shook her head.

"Scientific vessels travel here. Sometimes cruise ships. But private yachts like that one?" Doratea shook her head again. "That should not be here."

The yacht was too far away to see who was inside. But I knew. It was . . .

Fran Kenstein

Chapter 7

I quickly told Doratea all about Fran.

"I had planned for us to land and search for Roberto together," said Doratea. "But from what you say, I do not think we want this Señorita Kenstein to join us."

I definitely agreed with that.

"So we need a new plan," said Doratea. "How will we get to Roberto? First, I will drop you off with the map. Next, I will fly over the ship to lead Señorita Kenstein away. Then, I will fly back and join you. And that's how we will get to Roberto.

"Now," she added, "are you ready to jump out of this airplane?"

I was too surprised by the question to answer.

"Great!" she nodded, as if I had said yes. "Count down with me . . . *cinco, cuatro, tres, dos, uno, go!*"

"Wait, you want me to jump out of this plane right now?!" I exclaimed.

"No, I wanted you to do it when I told you to GO!" she replied. "But now will have to do."

With one sharp kick, Doratea shoved me out of the plane with her boot.

"Stay where you land. I will meet you as soon as I draw Señorita Kenstein away!" she yelled as I fell. "*Hasta luego, amigo!*"

At least, that's what I think she said. I was too busy looking at the white ground rushing up at me.

A hot jolt of panic spread down my arms.

It warmed the inside of the parka the explorers had given me, even though I was falling through air that was way below freezing.

WHOOOMP! Suddenly, I got a mouthful of snow as I face-planted in the tundra. But Doratea had brought me in just low enough. I was okay.

I got to my feet. From where I was standing, all I could see was snow and ice.

As I tried to think of what to do, a loud, rattling noise kept distracting me. I looked around for where that noise was coming from. And then I realized it was my teeth chattering.

I was  Freezing

Just as I was starting to feel sorry for myself, I remembered my cousin. He had been lost out here for who knows how long.

If I was freezing, he was probably feeling worse.

A lot worse.

I opened my journal to where I had stuffed the copy of Robert's map. There were a dozen paths traced on it. I had no idea which Robert had taken. I also didn't know how long it would take Doratea to come back. If I waited for her to start looking, it could be a long time before we found him.

I didn't know if he had that long.

Each path was marked with a different symbol — a pickaxe, a pile of coconuts, a canteen. I didn't know what they meant. And yet, there was something familiar. But what? If one of the symbols was reminding me of something I'd seen, there was probably a clue on one of the pages of my journal.

And that's when it hit me. Robert's email! Doratea had shown up right after the explorer handed it to me at the club. Things had been so rushed, I had shoved it into my journal and forgotten all about it. It had to have the clue I needed.

My hands were shaking with excitement (or maybe
frostbite) as I read it:

FROM: ROBERT.PERCY@EXPLORERS.NET
TO:< EMAIL@EXPLORERS.NET>
SUBJECT: HULLO!

HULLO FELLOW EXPLORERS CLUB MEMBERS!

I can't be sure when you will remember to check your
email, so I may already be safely back at home by the
time you read this.

Tomorrow, I'll be leaving the Eastern Antarctic
Research Station, on my trek to the last unexplored
spot on this beautiful continent. It should only take me
a day or so to get there.

The hard part is finding the right path to take. But
that's exactly what I've done! To celebrate, I'm
sending you this photo as I set out on my historic
journey!

Cheerio!

Robert

Robert was holding a glass of champagne in the photo. Was that the clue I was looking for? On his map, one of the trails was marked with a canteen. That wasn't exactly a glass of champagne, but it was pretty close!

I raced to follow that path. With my big feet, it was kinda like having a pair of snowshoes, and I made good time across the snow. Pretty soon, I came across some footprints. I'd done it!

Yeah, I'd done it all right — I had managed to get myself completely lost!

The footprints I had found were mine. Somehow, I had gotten turned around and crisscrossed my own tracks. I wasn't on the right path. The champagne glass in the photo hadn't been a clue after all.

And just as I realized I had no idea where I was, it started to snow. Hard.

"Don't panic," I told myself. "I'll figure something out." But all I could think was: what was I thinking?

I was no explorer! I had trouble following a map to get across my hometown! Which it looked like I'd probably never see again.

I didn't know how far I was from where Doratea told me to wait for her. I'd probably freeze before she could find me.

A **WHOOSH** of wind and ice ripped past me.

I may not have been an explorer,
but I knew a blizzard when I felt one.

Snow poured down on my journal, soaking the pages.

I knew what I had to do. I wrapped up my journal
as carefully as I could and buried it deep in the snow.
Maybe someone else would find it and the map —
someone who could figure out what object marked the
right way to go.

UGH

Chapter 8

Marked the right way to go! That was it! That was what I remembered!

I dug up the journal as quickly as I could. In the article, I read about Robert's trip to the tropical island . . . Yes! There it was!

When Robert had explored the island, he had used coconuts to mark the right way to go!

"'I lived on bananas and used coconuts to mark the right way to go,' said the explorer Robert Percy."

I opened the map. One of the dotted lines was marked with coconuts! That had to be the right path.

I had been right that the clue I needed was on one of the pages in my journal. I just picked the wrong page before.

It stopped snowing as I followed the coconut path on the map. It led me up a large mound of snow that gave me a view of the icy shore.

And that's where I saw Robert, bobbing up and down in the water.

His lower half was covered by a refrigerator-sized block of ice. His head and chest stuck out of the top of the ice block, allowing him to breath. But his arms and legs were pinned inside the hunk of ice. He was trapped.

I couldn't believe it. I'd done it! I'd found him! I'd had to come all the way to Antarctica, but I'd finally found a member of my family!

I raced down the other side of the mound, straight toward Robert.

As I ran, I thought of what I would say to him. I wanted to make a good first impression for once. So I tried to think of just the right thing to say to break the ice.

But then . . . the ice broke!

"WHHHULP!" I cried as the sheet of ice I was running down cracked and sent me sliding on my back with my legs in the air.

I clutched at the ice around me, but it was too slick. I couldn't stop myself.

I was heading feet first right toward the freezing water.

"Hullo there!" shouted Robert cheerily as I slid toward him. "Not to be a bother, but you had better stop yourself before you splash in here, or I dare say you'll end up an ice cube like me! How about you put your barking huge clodhoppers to good use!"

"**MY WHAT**?" I shouted.

"Your large feet," said Robert. "Put them down to get some traction."

I put my feet flat against the ice. I started to slow down. I stopped right at the water's edge.

"Thanks!" I gasped.

"Jolly good of the old boys at the club to finally send an explorer to rescue me," said Robert. "Even if you are a bit of a peculiar-looking one."

"I get my looks from my dad," I told him proudly. "But I'm no explorer."

I told him my whole story.

I told him everything I'd written in here up to now (even the embarrassing parts — he was family, after all). I told him how I hitched a ride with Doratea so I could find him, because I was the son of Frankenstein's Monster and was looking for my family. I told him how I was related to him through his father's feet. "Which makes you my cousin," I said.

Robert just looked at me. The only noise for miles was the lapping of the water on the ice.

That's when I realized how crazy I must have sounded. I had just come halfway around the world (Or was it more than that? I didn't even know!) to find him. And now he wouldn't even believe we were related!

There was only one thing to do. I started untying my boots.

"What are you doing?" he asked.

"I want to show you my feet!" I said. "I can prove we're related!"

He just looked at me, even more confused. "My dear boy, why would you do that?" he asked. "Of course we're related!

"The very first person to ever find his way to this place was me." He smiled proudly. "You, my boy, are the second. If that doesn't prove you've got the blood of an explorer in you, I don't know what will!"

I didn't think I could feel any happier than I felt right then. Until I heard the familiar **RMMMMMM** of Doratea's plane circling over the water!

Minutes later, the seaplane splashed down a hundred yards or so off shore. **CRUNK!** The cockpit door popped open and a rubber raft flopped out.

But Doratea didn't jump out of the plane and onto the raft.

Fran did!

OH NO!

Chapter 9

"**HHHHRRUNH!**" I grunted as I tried to pull Robert out of the water. The block of ice probably weighed a thousand pounds. And I had to be careful not to slip, or else I'd end up Popsicled too.

It was no use. And Fran was getting closer.

"Where's Doratea?" Robert shouted at her. "What did you do to her?"

"Not as much as I would have liked," said Fran with a creepy smile. "She had a surprising number of items in that little purple backpack of hers.

"Creepy Smile"

"But no matter," continued Fran as she motored closer. "I left your friend floating in the ocean. She cannot help you now."

I stopped pulling. There was no way I was getting Robert out of the water. And even if I did, it wasn't like I could carry him in that huge block of ice.

But there was no way I was leaving him. Not after waiting my whole life to find him.

There was only one thing to do. Just as Fran's raft hit the shore, I leaped at the water . . . and landed on Robert's block of ice! Bracing myself with my big feet, I didn't slide off. Instead, my momentum pushed us out to sea.

Right toward the plane!

"Good show!" exclaimed Robert.

Fran growled and raced after us in her boat.

I stuck my big feet in the water and kicked.

We had a lead, but she was gaining.

"When we get to the plane, you won't be able to get me inside like this," Robert said matter-of-factly. I guess to an explorer being ridden like a boat while being chased by the crazy daughter of Dr. Frankenstein wasn't anything to get too worked up about. "You'll have to tie me to one of the pontoons."

Fran was just yards behind us when we reached the plane. I flung open the cockpit door and climbed in, my feet instantly turning to Popsicles as soon as I took them out of the water. I quickly found a rope. But as I tied Robert's block to the pontoon, I suddenly realized: "Wait! Who's going to fly the plane!?!"

"You are!" he said cheerily.

"Me?" I cried. "I don't know how! There's no way I can fly a plane!"

"It's the duty of explorers to go where people think they cannot," said Robert. "Even if the people who think that are themselves!"

Fran was right there, reaching with a knife to cut Robert loose. I didn't know which button to push. So I pushed them all. The windshield wipers wiped. The wing flaps flapped. The lights lit up.

And then, I just barely heard Fran curse me as the engine roared to life and drowned her out.

Woooooo!

A couple days later, I got an email from Robert.

FROM: ROBERT.PERCY@EXPLORERS.NET
TO:< EMAIL@EXPLORERS.NET>
SUBJECT: HULLO!

Hullo cousin!

Just landed the plane to refuel at the research station and found a computer I could borrow for a few minutes. I've been searching day and night since I dropped you on the mainland. No luck finding Doratea yet, but I know I will.

Despite the smashing escape we made, I can tell Ms. Kenstein isn't the type who will just give up and call it a day. Now that I know to look out for her, I'm confident I can throw a spanner in the works if she comes after me again.

But you need to warn the rest of your cousins before Ms. Kenstein can find them. I'm certain you will, even if you need to go to the ends of the Earth to do so.

You've got the blood of an explorer in you, just like me. When adventure calls, you go feet first!

But you already know that. What I wanted to tell you is that I have never been on an adventure like the one I had with you. My dad died before I was old enough to go exploring with him. This was my first adventure with family.

But not the last. As soon as I find Doratea, I plan to join you on your quest to find the rest of your family. And by that time, Doratea will be family too — the first thing I'm going to do when I see her is plan our wedding immediately.

I hope you're chuffed by the news, old boy! You thought you had only found one cousin so far, but you've actually met two!

Cheerio!

Robert

I had a big smile on my face as I taped Robert's email to a blank page in my journal.

It was still a little cold and soggy from the Antarctic waters, but all the pages I had from Dr. Frankenstein's journal were still inside.

And somewhere out there, Fran was looking for the rest of my cousins. But I knew nothing bad would happen to them . . .

Because I Was going to find them First!

NEXT...

WHOSE EYES?

I for an Eye

Chapter 10

I was standing on the corner of Spring and Second
Streets when the whole city of Los Angeles shook!

As the ground **RRRRUMBLED**,
I grabbed the mailbox next to me and wished
everything would just stop moving!

And then it did.

That's when I realized I'd just survived my first
earthquake. It had only lasted a second or two. It
must have been a really small one on the Rictor or
Richter or whatever-you-call-it scale.

Nothing was damaged and no one was hurt.

In fact, no one else seemed to notice the
earthquake at all. I guess here in Los Angeles,
little earthquakes like that one were pretty normal.
Everyone around me just kept driving or walking.

The only thing that seemed weird to them was me.

That wasn't too surprising. Anyone who's met me
knows I can make a pretty odd first impression.

Maybe it's because my feet are too big for
my legs. Or because my left hand is way bigger
than my right. Or because one eye is blue
and the other is bright green.

Or maybe it's because I'm the son of . . .

FRANKENSTEIN'S MONSTER!

Not that any of the people passing me in downtown
Los Angeles knew that. I had only just found that out
myself.

I never knew my dad, but I had read about him. I'd only bothered to print out one of the newspaper articles I'd found and taped it here in my journal, because they were all pretty much the same.

Apparently, my dad tended to freak people out.

FRANKENSTEIN'S MONSTER

Note to my future self: If you've forgotten the rest of that story — and I can't believe you ever would — just look back at the earlier part of this journal!

My journal was the most valuable thing I owned. Partly because it was pretty much the only thing I owned. But also because it contained every clue I had found about my cousins.

Taped inside it was every clue I had found about my cousins. Including the pages I had gotten from Dr. Frankenstein's journal.

Dr. F's journal told the story of how he created my dad. I only had copies of a few pages from it, but they were the best clues I had.

After my adventure with Robert, I had gone to stay with his friends at the Explorers Club.

They were so happy I had found Robert, they offered to get me anywhere in the world I wanted to go.

Now I just had to figure out where to go to find my next cousin.

The problem was, I didn't have Dr. Frankenstein's whole journal.

If I had had the whole thing, it would have been a lot easier to figure out where all the parts that went into my dad came from. But the only one who had the whole journal was Fran.

Fran Kenstein (crazy) was Dr. Frankenstein's daughter. She wanted to create a new monster. But there had been something special about the mix of body parts that went into my dad.

To build a new monster, Fran needed body parts with the same DNA. And the only way to get them was to take them from my cousins.

I had beaten her to Robert. Somehow or another, I had to get to the rest of my cousins and warn them about her before she could find them.

Sitting in the library at the Explorers Club, I kept looking at one page from Dr. Frankenstein's journal. It had a detailed drawing of one of my dad's eyes.

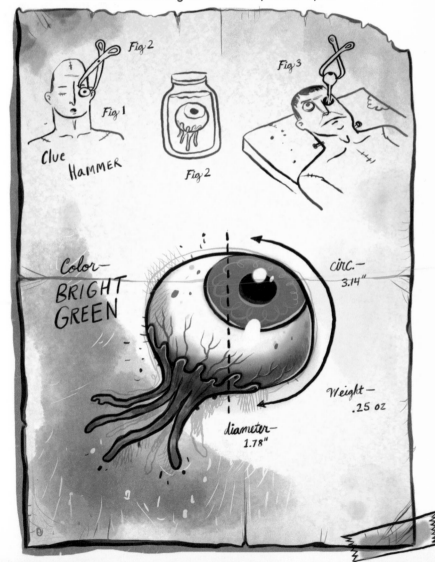

But who had Dr. Frankenstein taken it from?

I was sure there had to be a clue on this page. Mostly because the word "clue" was written on it.

GROSS!

"Clue Hammer." What did that mean? Was the hammer a clue? Was a clue hammer what Dr. Frankenstein used to get the eyeball out? (Ew!) Was there even a kind of tool called a "clue hammer"?

Borrowing the explorers' computer, I did a quick search. I learned that there was no such thing as a tool called a clue hammer. But there was a Samuel "Clue" Hammer! He was a famous private detective in Los Angeles in the 1940s.

I wasn't entirely sure what a private detective did. Was it different from being a public detective?

I kept clicking and reading what I found. Turns out, Samuel Hammer held the record for most cases solved in the history of Los Angeles (also, there was no such thing as a public detective).

I found a lot of photos of Samuel Hammer, but since they were from the 1940s, they were in black and white. I couldn't tell if he was the one the bright green eye came from.

Then I found an article from many years later, with a color photo of Samuel holding a baby. Both of them had bright green eyes!

The article didn't say much other than that the famous Samuel Hammer had a newborn grandson.

The only other article that mentioned the grandson was Samuel Hammer's obituary from a few years later.

The obituary also mentioned something else: the address and phone number of the detective agency Samuel Hammer worked for!

YES!

Even though Samuel wasn't around anymore, his office would have records or maybe even someone who had known him!

Either way, I'd be able to find his grandson — my second cousin!

The second cousin I'd found, that is. (Since he was related to me because his grandfather's eye was put into my dad, maybe that made him my "second cousin one eyeball removed"?)

I raced to the phone, but there was no answer when I called.

Maybe everyone in the office was out solving a crime or something.

I put down the phone and ran out the door.

It was the only lead I had. And if I had it, there was a good chance Fran had it too.

The explorers had promised to get me anywhere in the world I wanted to go. Now I knew exactly where that was.

Samuel Hammer's office in Los Angeles.

Sixteen hours later, I was crossing Spring Street in downtown LA.

Samuel's office was just around the corner.

I was so excited, I couldn't help but run the last block to the address. And then I saw it!

I was looking at an empty lot.

I had been in such a rush to follow the clue, I hadn't even taken the time to think about it.

Samuel Hammer had been a famous detective in the 1940s. That was like **80** years ago! It shouldn't have been a huge surprise his office wasn't there anymore.

That's why no one had answered the phone. The whole building was gone!

"Don't panic," I told myself again. "I'll figure something out."

But the only thing I could think of was "at least things can't get worse."

And then things got worse.

Fran Kenstein worse!

Fran was on the other side of the street!

Chapter 12

I ducked into the shadow of the building next
door. Fran didn't even glance my way. She was totally
focused on where she was going, walking quickly with
an evil smile on her face.

I had seen that smile before — when she had talked
about taking my cousins' body parts to build her
monster!

Was Fran following the same clue from Dr.
Frankenstein's journal as I was? Did she know how to
find Samuel Hammer's grandson? Was she on her way
to him now?

I had to find out.

OUCH!

I trailed her, or tailed her, or whatever you call it as she walked all the way down Grand Avenue. She walked so far that the sun set, and a full moon rose.

My huge feet were aching, but Fran kept walking faster and faster.

Fran marched right up to a building that covered an entire block. Metal letters on top of the building spelled out the words "Los Angeles Convention Center."

Fran pushed her way through a glass door. I counted to three and followed her inside. And ran right into a man-sized badger!

BADGER

There were dozens — no, hundreds — of people-sized animals walking around in there!

Were they victims of one of Fran's insane experiments? What had she done to them?

What would they do to me?

I slowly backed my way toward the door. That's when I saw the banner hanging from the ceiling. It read, "The Los Angeles Convention Center Welcomes You to THE PROFESSIONAL SPORTS MASCOT CONVENTION!"

Okay, whew! These weren't half-human animals. Or even half-animal humans. They were people in mascot costumes! I recognized the dolphin from that football team. And the dinosaur from that basketball team. I wasn't sure what the orange fuzzy thing with the big yellow nose was supposed to be, but I knew I had seen it on TV.

It was actually pretty cool.

Or would have been, if it weren't for Fran.

She still hadn't seen me in the crowd. She was too busy looking for someone else.

Which could only mean one thing . . . One of my cousins was inside one of these mascot costumes!

If Fran was following the same clue from Dr. Frankenstein's journal as I was, she had to be looking for Samuel Hammer's grandson.

But which one was he?

The mascots were covered from head to toe by their costumes. All you could see of the person underneath were their eyes.

Fran looked at costume after costume. But she didn't see what she was looking for. Frustrated, she moved deeper into the sprawling convention center.

And that's when I saw him. He was standing near the men's room, dressed as a grouper. Or maybe a marlin. Definitely some kind of blue fish.

His eyes were focused on a man dressed as a blue jay. Maybe that's what made me notice the bright green in the eyeholes of the fish head.

The same bright green eyes as Samuel Hammer! The same bright **GREEN** as my left eye!

I'd found him!

Now I just had to make sure Fran didn't.

As soon as Fran was out of sight, I raced up to my cousin.

I didn't know how long I had before Fran wandered back. I had to warn him now.

"There's something I've got to tell you right away," I said. "You're the grandson of Samuel Hammer, the famous detective, right?"

"Shh! Quiet!" whispered the man in the fish costume. "Did the Chief send you?"

"Chief?" I asked, confused. "Wait, you mean that Indian Chief mascot over there? No, I . . . well, this is kind of hard to explain, but my name's J.D. and —"

"Look, that's swell. But can you scram?" he replied. "Don't mean to give you the bum's rush, but I'm kind of busy here."

"Actually, no," I told him. "This can't wait. See, there's this girl named Fran Kenstein who is hunting for my cousins. So if you're the grandson of Samuel Hammer, the famous detective —"

"Detective? Who's a detective?!" cried a man dressed in a blue jay costume. He had been about to go into the men's room. Instead, he took off running for the exit.

"Thanks, kid!" sighed my cousin.

"You're welcome," I replied.

"No, I meant everything's all wet because of you!" he exclaimed. "I'm a detective, just like my granddad. And I'm undercover on a case! I was following that guy in the blue jay costume!"

"Oh," was all I could think to say.

The detective reached inside his fish costume and pulled out a police walkie-talkie.

"All units near the convention center, this is Detective Sam Hammer of the MCU! Requesting backup! Suspect on the run!" he said into his walkie-talkie. "Suspect is approximately six feet tall and dressed as a blue jay. Over!"

The detective put his walkie-talkie down and slipped out of his costume. "The two-time loser inside that blue jay costume is a hood named Lavenza," he said to me. "I've been tailing him for days. Lavenza's a thug for hire. Big-time crooks call him when they are planning some very bad business. He was just pretending to be a mascot to meet the criminal who wanted to hire him."

The detective looked at the bathroom Lavenza had been about to enter. "Which means that palooka is probably in there!"

The detective put his hand on the bathroom door. "Stay out here," he warned me. "It could get dangerous in there."

He was right. Only the danger didn't stay inside!

A man in a wolf costume slashed through the door with his claws!

He knocked the detective over.

And then he ran right at **ME!!**

CREEPY!

Chapter 13

All I saw was hair.

The man running at me was covered in it. He was so furry, the hair covered the blue suit with square buttons that he was wearing. He raced right past me and disappeared into the crowd.

"Are you okay?" the detective asked.

"Yeah," I nodded. "I don't know how he could move so fast in that costume."

"Hooey! That was no costume," he said. "Could costume claws do this?"

The detective pointed to the bathroom door — or what was left of it. It was shredded.

"That," said the detective, "was the Werewolf! I've been trying to bust that mug for months. Now shake a leg! We gotta catch him!"

He grabbed my big left hand and dragged me into the crowd after him.

"We?" I asked. "I'm no detective! I don't know the first thing about detecting. Wait, is that even a word? See! I don't even know that."

"I didn't get a look at him, kid," said the detective. "I'll need you to help me spot him."

"Um, don't you think a hairy Werewolf will kind of stand out in a crowd?" I asked as I tried to keep up with him.

"In this crowd?" he replied. "No dice."

The convention floor was packed with hundreds of people dressed as lions, tigers, and every other animal you could think of.

Including wolves. **RRRRR!**

It was probably the only place on the planet the Werewolf could walk around without being noticed. Which must have been why he picked it.

"My name's Sam, by the way," said the detective as we ran past penguins, sharks, and falcons, looking for the Werewolf. "Sam Hammer the Third. Say, how'd you know I was here undercover?"

"I didn't," I told him. "I just recognized your bright green eyes."

"You got the eye of a detective, kid," he said, impressed. "And I should know. I inherited mine from my grandfather."

"I think I inherited mine from him too," I replied.

As we made our way through the crowd, I told him my story. I took out my journal and showed him the drawing of his grandfather's eye. Which went into my dad. Which made us related.

Sam didn't even bat a green eye. "When you put it like that, I guess that does make us related," he said. "I'm not surprised. You definitely followed the clues to me like a born detective."

"I don't know about that. I'm just lucky I found you," I told him. "I knew about your grandfather, but there was hardly anything online about you."

Sam's face turned red.

"That's because I haven't cracked any cases big enough to get in the papers," he said. "Not yet. But I will. I learned everything I know about being a gumshoe from my granddad. Including how to flap my gums."

"Flap your gums?" I asked.

Sam shrugged. "That's how detectives in the 1940s used to say 'talk,'" he told me. "And if it was good enough for my granddad, it's swell enough for me."

I didn't ask him why people in the 1940s said "flap your gums" when it was a lot easier just to say "talk." It was probably the same reason people in the Middle Ages said "thou" instead of "you." Or why people used to ride horses instead of cars.

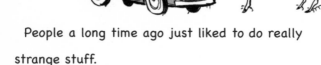

People a long time ago just liked to do really strange stuff.

"No gumshoe in this city of angels ever cracked more cases than my granddad did," said Sam. "I've spent my whole life trying to be as great a detective as he was. And until I do, I'm not gonna stop!"

And then he stopped.

We had reached the end of the convention center. There was no sign of the Werewolf.

Sam took out his walkie-talkie.

"This is Detective Hammer of the MCU," he shouted into the walkie-talkie. "I'm in pursuit of the second suspect. He may have left the building. All units, be on the lookout for the Werewolf. Description — hair: long. Claws: sharp."

Then Sam saw something through the crowd. His face went white.

"What is it?" I asked. "Is it the Werewolf?"

"No dice. It's much worse than that," said Sam. "It's my boss."

Chapter 14

The Chief of Police marched up. He was followed by several policemen. They had the man in the blue jay costume in tow.

"Let me do the gum flapping," Sam told me. "You take that notebook or journal or whatever it is in your back pocket and draw the Werewolf. You had the best look at him. I want you to draw as many details before you forget them."

The Chief's dress uniform was blue. His gloves were white. His face was red. A very angry red.

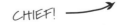

CHIEF! ——→

"I can explain, Chief," Sam started.

"No!" roared the Chief. "I'm going to explain
something to YOU! I shouldn't have to remind you of
this, but you're a detective in the MCU," roared the
Chief. "That stands for the Monster Crimes Unit! That
means you're supposed to investigate monster crimes.
You know, crimes committed by the Mummy or the
Vampire — guys like that."

Holy crud!

monster crimes!

Did that mean Sam had run into my dad?

Now didn't seem like a good time to ask. Sam was
too busy being yelled at by the Chief.

"Lavenza is not a monster!" the Chief shouted as
he pointed at the man in the blue jay costume. "He's
just a crook in a silly bird costume. And it's not even
a monster costume! That means it's not your job to go
after him!"

Then the Chief turned to the police officers holding Lavenza. "Take him back to headquarters and put him in a cell. I'll figure out what to do with him later."

The policemen took Lavenza away, leaving the Chief behind.

"But this was a monster crime, sir," Sam insisted. "Lavenza only works for criminals who are planning big crimes. And he was here to meet the Werewolf! They're in cahoots!"

The Chief groaned. "Here we go again with the Werewolf! You've been talking about him for months! But you've never been able to find a single shred of evidence that he even exists."

"I know, but this time I've got an eyewitness who got a good look at him!" Sam said. "J.D., show the Chief what you saw."

I handed the Chief my journal, open to the page where I had drawn the Werewolf.

BUTTONS,
LOTS OF HAIR,
AND CLAWS!

The Chief studied the picture. "Oh, okay, now I see," he said. Then he roared, "I see a child's drawing of some guy covered in fur. Which describes pretty much everyone here! You probably just saw someone in a wolf costume.

"Look, Sam," said the Chief in a gentler voice, "I know how important it is to you to live up to your grandfather's legend. He was a great detective. The greatest, in fact. But this isn't your case. Because it's not a monster crime. If Lavenza was here to meet another criminal, leave it to the regular cops to figure out who it was."

"Actually," said a voice from the crowd. "You don't have to leave it to anyone. I can tell you exactly who it was."

Oh, no — I recognized that voice. It was Fran! She smiled as she walked up to the Chief.

"Don't listen to her!" I told the Chief.   UGH!

"I give orders. I don't take them!" scowled the Chief. "Now what are you talking about?" he asked Fran.

"That peculiar-looking boy!" said Fran, pointing at me. "He must be a criminal! I saw him with the man in the blue jay costume. They were talking together. It looked like they were plotting something!"

"Is that so?" said the Chief, turning to me.

"NO, IT'S NOT!" I said.

"I trust the boy, Chief," Sam insisted.

"And why is that?" asked the Chief. "Do you know him?"

"Yes," Sam said. "Well, we just met a few minutes ago. But he's my cousin. Well, not technically. But —"

"I see," interrupted the Chief. He turned to me. "What's your name?" the Chief asked.

"J.D.," I stammered.

"Last name?" he asked.

"It's just J.D.," I told him. "It stands for John Doe."

"I see," he scowled. "And what is your address?"

"Well, since I left the orphanage, I don't exactly have one," I admitted.

"Hmm . . . a John Doe with no known address," the Chief said to Sam. "And that doesn't sound at all suspicious?"

"Well, I can see how that might sound a little hinky," Sam admitted.

The Chief turned to Fran. "Thank you for coming forward," the Chief told her.

"Only too happy to help," she beamed.

"Wait, you can't believe what she says!" I said. "You don't know who she is!"

"My name is Fran Kenstein," Fran told the Chief.

Fran held out her wallet. "Here is my ID with my address."

"Now I know who SHE is," the Chief said to me, "which is more than I can say for you, John Doe with no known address.

"You see, Sam?" the Chief told Sam. "Just like I told you, this isn't a case for the Monster Crimes Unit. Lavenza was here to meet this kid! But I'll tell you what. Since you're so eager to be involved, I'll let you bring the boy back to HQ so he can be processed."

Something bounced against the inside of my shirt. I looked down and realized it was my heart! I was going to jail!

YIKES!

How could the Chief believe Fran? If he only knew what she was really like . . .

But of course he didn't. Only I did. Well, Fran did too. But she wasn't telling.

"I would take him in myself," the Chief continued, "but I'm late for a haircut. When I get back, I want to see him in a cell!"

"But Chief —" Sam started.

CHOP
CHOP

"The only thing I want to hear from you is 'Yes, sir!'" barked the Chief. "I don't care if your grandfather was Samuel Hammer. If you don't follow my orders, I'll make sure you never work as a detective in Los Angeles again!"

Sam's face went white. "Yes, sir," he mumbled.

"Good," said the Chief. Then he turned to Fran. "Thank you again for your time."

"It was my pleasure." She smiled.

"I had been in a hurry to visit someone," she said as she looked at Sam. Then she turned to me and added darkly: "Actually several someones. But it looks like I now have all the time in the world to do that. There won't be anything getting in my way anymore."

I tried to think of something to say to her. But it was kind of hard to think when Sam was CLICKING handcuffs around my wrists.

The Chief nodded to Sam, then escorted Fran out of the building.

CLICK   CLICK

"Okay," I told myself. "Don't panic. You'll think of something."

And, you know what, I did think of something.

I thought, **"I AM SO DOOMED!"**

Chapter 15

"You can't do this!" I pleaded with Sam. "If I'm locked up, who is going to warn my other cousins about Fran?"

"You heard what the Chief said," said Sam.

And then he unlocked my cuffs! HUH?!?!

"The Chief said he expects to see you behind bars when he gets back to the office," said the detective. "So I'd say that gives us two hours tops to pinch the Werewolf and prove the Chief gave you a bum rap. So let's shake a leg!"

Sam led me back to the bathroom door the Werewolf had shredded.

"What a bunch of hooey!" Sam said, shaking his head. "The Chief is so sure you were the one meeting Lavenza, he didn't leave anyone to search for clues the Werewolf might have left. That means it's up to us, J.D.!"

I followed Sam as he went into the bathroom and started looking around.

"I don't know why the Chief didn't believe me." Sam sighed. "But he's always looked down on the Monster Crimes Unit."

"Oh, man! In all the excitement about going to jail and my life being over, I totally forgot! You're in the Monster Crimes Unit!" I said. "That means you know all about monsters!"

"MONSTERS LIKE MY DAD!"

"Well, yes and no," said Sam as he searched the bathroom for clues. "The Vampire, the Mummy, the Fishman from the Dark Lagoon — when mugs like that get into some bad business, then yeah, I catch the case. But Frankenstein's Monster never committed any crime in Los Angeles. At least as far as I know. He was a bit before my time. He disappeared years before I became a gumshoe."

I guess he could see I was disappointed he couldn't tell me more about my dad.

"But that doesn't mean I can't help you find out about him," Sam added quickly. "I am a gumshoe after all. As soon as we pinch the Werewolf, I promise, I'll — holy mazuma!"

Sam had been digging through the trash can next to the sink. Now he started digging even faster. "I found something!" he exclaimed. "Look!"

In Sam's hands were ripped-up pieces of paper.

"You found some trash in the trash can? What's so strange about that?" I asked.

"This isn't trash. It's a clue! A really swell clue! This paper wasn't ripped. It was shredded. See the cut marks on the edges? You'll find the same marks on the door," he said. "Because they were both shredded by the Werewolf's claws!"

I looked. He was right!

 ← EEEEK!

"The Werewolf must have tried to destroy this when he heard us outside," Sam said as he collected more pieces of paper. "Now let's put this back together and see what it says!"

We got to work piecing the paper back together. Unfortunately, it turned out werewolf claws were really good at shredding! We couldn't find all the pieces, but we taped what we found onto a page in my journal (good thing I kept some tape — as well as a couple of pens — in my back pocket with my journal).

Lavenza,

The Crime is tonight.
we start at
We will meet at
near the   where the
we are going to steal is

If there are any   there
we will
If the police   , we will
even if that means firing
the
I will supply the guns for us
to   if

"There's a lot missing, but these are definitely instructions for the crime the Werewolf's plotting tonight!" said Sam. "He must have been planning to give this to Lavenza. But he never got the chance!

"And look at this," said Sam, pointing to what looked like part of a necklace of circles at the top of the page. "That symbol looks familiar. I can't remember where I've seen it, though. Somewhere back at HQ. Maybe in the Werewolf's police file."

EVIDENCE?

"Then let's go! We gotta show this to the Chief of Police," I exclaimed excitedly. "It proves the Werewolf was the one Lavenza was here to meet."

Sam shook his head. "I don't see where this is signed by the Werewolf, do you?" he asked. "In fact, it doesn't mention the Werewolf anywhere. This doesn't prove squat. Anyone could have written this. Including you, J.D.

"At least, that's what the Chief of Police would say," he finished.

I slumped. We were no closer to figuring this out than when we started!

"Just because a clue doesn't tell you everything doesn't mean it's telling you nothing," Sam said. "Sometimes, a sleuth just needs someone to give him a little more information to put the puzzle together."

"That's great," I replied. "But who's going to give us more information?"

"The Werewolf," Sam said with a smile.

NO WAY!

Chapter 16

Sam led me through the convention center to a room marked "Video Surveillance."

Sam showed his badge to the man inside. He left and Sam sat down at the controls in front of a big monitor.

"I'm pulling up the footage from when we saw the Werewolf," Sam told me. "That's going to take a minute or two."

While I waited, I took out my journal and thought of everyone on the Chief's list of suspects.

Lavenza. Me.

That right there was my problem: how was I going to get my name off that list and the real criminal's name on it?

Of course, there was one easy way to do that. I took out my pen and wrote:

That didn't really change anything. Well, not true — it did change one thing. It made me feel a little better. Just a little.

Sam saw what I had written.

"That should be Werewolf," said Sam. "Not Wolfman."

"What's the difference?" I asked.

"Well, for starters, a Wolfman is a man," said Sam. "We don't know if the Werewolf is a guy or a dame. Even if it is a he, he could be anybody."

"Or anywhere," I sighed.

"That's what we are here to narrow down," said Sam. "Take a look at these."

Sam laid out a bunch of printouts from the convention center's main surveillance camera.

They all looked pretty much the same to me: they each showed the entire convention floor crowded with sports mascots.

The only difference was the time printed on the bottom of the photos.

"This camera takes a photo of the entire convention floor every sixty seconds. These were taken from the time the Werewolf ran from us until now," Sam explained. "If we can see which exit he ankled out of, it may give us a clue as to where he went."

I nodded and took half of the stack of pictures to look through. Each one had dozens of furry costumed mascots.

Looking for the Werewolf in that crowd was like trying to find a needle in a furstack.

So I was pretty surprised when I spotted him (or maybe her?) right away!

"Aces!" Sam smiled. "You really do have the eye of a gumshoe! There's the Werewolf, right there, going into that bathroom right in the middle of the convention center!

"What is it with the Werewolf and bathrooms?" Sam wondered, trying to figure out if it were some kind of clue.

"Maybe he isn't housebroken?" I offered.

Sam didn't answer. He was busy shuffling through the rest of the printouts.

DON'T FORGET TO FLUSH

"Look at this," said Sam. "This is the picture taken a minute later. There's the Chief already here, pretty close to where the Werewolf was in your photo. If the Werewolf had left the bathroom then, the Chief would have seen him for sure."

Sam pulled out the rest of the photos and looked through them quickly. There was no sign of the Werewolf in any of them.

"Which means," said Sam, "the Werewolf never came out of that bathroom!"

A minute later, Sam and I were standing outside of that bathroom.

"This could get pretty hairy," Sam said. "Better let me go first."

I didn't argue with that.

Sam charged in. It was hairy, all right. Very hairy!

There was hair everywhere in the bathroom.

But there was no Werewolf. Or anyone else. The bathroom was empty, except for the fur everywhere.

And the disposable razor and can of shaving cream on the sink.

"Of course!" said Sam as he picked up the shaving cream. "We never saw the Werewolf come out of the bathroom because he shaved off all his hair!

"But that would leave him naked," Sam continued, thinking it through. "Unless he had clothes somewhere . . ."

"He had clothes," I said, thinking, "when he ran past me. Under all his hair he was wearing some kind of blue suit."

"That answers that," Sam nodded. "He'd still have his claws, though. But he could easily have hidden them in his pockets. Or in a pair of gloves.

"In which case," Sam continued, "the Werewolf would have come out of here looking like he normally does. And since we don't know what that looks like, this is a —"

"Dead end." I sighed.

OH CRUD!

"Good gumshoes don't let dead ends stop them," said Sam. "When they hit one, they change directions and keep going."

"How are we supposed to keep going?" I asked. "We don't know where to go!"

"We don't know where the Werewolf is," Sam said, "but there's one hood we do know where to find."

I smiled. "Lavenza!" The Chief had told the policemen to take him back to headquarters and put him in a cell.

"If we get him to sing," Sam said, nodding, "he may be the one to piece this puzzle together!"

The Los Angeles Police Department headquarters was cube-shaped building of glittering glass.

Most boys my age would have been psyched to have been personally invited there by the Chief of Police.

Of course, my invitation was more like a one-way ticket. Which actually turned out to be a good thing.

When the officers at the front desk asked what I was doing there, Sam told them the Chief had ordered him to take me to the holding cells.

By the looks on their faces, I could tell most of them were too scared of the Chief to call and ask him. But if any of them did, the Chief would have told them that Sam was telling the truth.

So that was one good thing about the Chief wanting me locked up, I guess.

"Watch your beezer," Sam warned as we walked down the hallway toward the holding cells.

"Got it," I nodded back. Then I whispered, "Wait, my beezer is my back right?"

"Nope, your nose," Sam said.

"That was totally my next guess," I lied.

Lavenza was sitting in his cell, still wearing his blue jay costume.

← JAILBIRD! HA!

"All right, jailbird," said Sam. "I need you to sing."

Lavenza leaped up. "Sure!" He nodded eagerly. "I'll tell you anything I know. I don't like jail. I just want to get out of here!"

"Swell," said Sam. "So look here, we found the note the Werewolf was going to give you —"

"Wait, the Werewolf?" interrupted Lavenza. "Was that who was trying to hire me? I only talked to him once on the phone. I never got to meet him." Lavenza looked at me. "That kid blew your cover, and I ran before I could."

"Never mind that," said Sam. "I want to know about the Werewolf's plan. Spill!"

"I can't!" moaned Lavenza.

"Don't be a sap," Sam told him. "Don't you want out of here?"

"I do!" cried Lavenza. "But I can't tell you his plan, because I don't know what he was planning! All I know is I got a call from some guy, asking me to help him pull some big crime. I didn't know it was the Werewolf. He told me to rent this costume and meet him at the mascot convention so he could fill me in on the crime.

"But I never got to meet him," he wailed. "Because of you!"

Sam turned to me. He didn't say it, but I knew what he was thinking.

Another dead end.

DEAD END ← NOT AGAIN!

We were running out of leads — and out of time. In fact, we were down to our very last lead: that necklace of circles on the top of the note the Werewolf had written for Lavenza.

Sam told me to wait in the detective's lunchroom while he got the Werewolf's file to see if that's where he had seen that symbol before.

"At this time of night, no one should come in here," he said as he left me in the bathroom. "But just in case, lock the door until I come back."

As I waited for Sam, I took out my journal and started writing down what had happened. I didn't get very far before there was a light knock at the door. Sam was back, carrying two thick folders.

"Here's the file on the Werewolf," said Sam, patting the folder he held under one arm. "And here's one for you," he said, tossing another file on the table.

Sam went to a vending machine and threw in a handful of quarters. He offered me half of what came out of the slot, but I shook my head.

EWW!

I was hungry, but not hungry enough to eat a stale avocado sandwich.

Not when I had the LAPD's file on Frankenstein's Monster sitting on the table in front of me!

Inside could be the answer to every question I ever had about my dad!

And maybe a whole bunch of clues to finding my other cousins!

"Like I said, your dad was before my time," Sam told me as he crunched loudly on his sandwich. "But in that file is everything the police ever found out about him."

I opened the file to the cover page.

But before I could get any farther, Sam cried out: "You gotta be kidding me! What a load of bunk!

"There's nothing in the Werewolf's file!" he exclaimed. "Look! It's just stuffed with blank pages! Someone took everything out!"

"Maybe it was another detective in the Monster Crimes Unit?" I suggested. "Maybe he took it to the copy machine or something?"

Sam shook his head. "I'm the only detective in the Monster Crimes Unit. And if the Chief had his way, there wouldn't even be me."

"So then who could have taken it?" I asked.

"I don't know, kid," he said. "Detectives aren't allowed to touch files that aren't in their department. Not without special permission from someone way high up."

I turned back to my dad's file.

If I was going to jail, at least I could go with answers to all my questions about him. But I didn't get past the cover page.

Because I saw it!

What we had been looking for was right there!

In the middle of the cover sheet was the LAPD logo.

JUN 9. 93
AUG 2. 56
MONSTER CRIMES UNIT
CONFIDENTIAL
FRANKENSTEIN'S MONSTER
LAPD
RESTRICTED MATERIAL
DEC 11. 77

If you covered up the top two-thirds of the logo, the bottom part that was left looked exactly like the "necklace" of circles we had seen on the note the Werewolf had shredded!

Sam slapped his forehead. "Of course!" he cried. "I can't believe I didn't recognize it! I had been trying to think of what criminal organization had a symbol like that. I never would have thought of something I see every day!"

Something BUZZED loudly.

"Hang on," Sam said. "I'm getting a call on my blower." He took out his walkie-talkie and hit a button.

A voice roared out the speaker: "Why isn't that kid behind bars?" shouted the Chief.

Chapter 18

Sam and I stood in the Chief's office, waiting for him to come out of his private bathroom.

And for life as I knew it to end.

As we stood there, I looked around. I guess I thought the Chief of Police would have had a fancy office, like a President or a CEO. But there actually wasn't much in it. Just a desk, a comfy chair, and a wastebasket.

Which was filled with disposable razors and empty cans of shaving cream!

The same kind we had found in the convention center bathroom where the Werewolf . . .

No. No Way!

That's when I noticed the Chief's blue uniform jacket hanging on a hook on the outside of the bathroom door.

It was the exact same blue as the suit I had seen under the Werewolf's fur.

The Chief's jacket was decorated with several medals. SQUARE medals. Which looked just like what I had thought were square buttons on the Werewolf's jacket!

Hang on. The Chief was the Werewolf?

If he were, it would explain why the note to Lavenza was written on paper with the police logo on it! And why when the Werewolf went into the convention center bathroom and shaved, we saw the Chief outside the bathroom a minute later!

Not to mention, the Chief was in the bathroom again right now! Which was like the Werewolf's favorite place to be!

"Sam!" I whispered. "You're not going to believe it, but I think —"

And that's when the door to the bathroom opened.

I clammed up fast.  ← HA!

As the Chief came out, I saw another disposable razor on the sink behind him. And there was a tuft of thick fur on the back of his neck! He had missed a spot with his razor!

There was no doubt about it. The Chief was the Werewolf.

And we were trapped in his office with him!

I couldn't risk saying anything to Sam. Not without at least letting the Chief know that I knew who he was first!

"This is not going to end well for you," the Chief growled at me.

Oh no! I waited for him to say "Because I know you know!" and then leap at me!

But instead he said, "Because you're about to go to jail for a long time."

Whew! I didn't think anyone had ever felt so relieved to hear they were going to jail!

"Chief, wait," said Sam.

"You're in enough trouble as it is, Detective! That boy should already be behind bars," said the Chief as he pointed a white-gloved finger at me.

Now that I knew what to look for, I could see there was something wrong about his fingers inside his white gloves. Because they weren't fingers at all.

They were claws!

"Sam, I'm really ready to go to jail right now!" I cried.

"Good," said the Chief. "Take him now, Sam. I've got somewhere I have to be."

The Chief got up to leave. Oh, crud! He must have been leaving to commit his crime!

I just wanted to get out of his office without the Chief turning his claws on me.

But the note he wrote to Lavenza said people might get hurt. Maybe even killed. I had to do something.

Maybe there was a way I could figure out what the Chief was planning to do. Without him figuring out what I was trying to do! Then I could fill Sam in when we were safely out of the Chief's reach. I didn't know if it would work, but I had to try.

So I turned to the Chief and tried to sound normal as I asked, "So, um, where are you off to?"

WOW! →

One of the Chief's bushy eyebrows moved an inch up his forehead. "Why would you want to know that?" he asked.

Well, because the shredded note said the Werewolf was going to strike tonight, but it didn't say where! But I couldn't tell the Chief that! Or else he'd surely shred me too!

"Go on, J.D.," Sam told me. "Answer the Chief."

Oh man! I guess Sam hadn't figured the Chief was the Werewolf!

"Show him your journal," said Sam, as he grabbed it out of my pocket. "Show him the surveillance photos from the convention center. The one that shows the Werewolf going into a bathroom and the other that shows the Chief showing up a minute later. Tell him how we found shaving cream and a razor in that bathroom. And how the Werewolf's file is gone, even though very few people have access to it."

Sam put my journal in my terror-frozen hands. Then he flipped through the pages, showing the Chief everything we had found.

"Oh, I'm sure the Chief doesn't want to see all this," I said nervously.

"Actually, I do," said the Chief, taking off his gloves.

"Sam, run!" I cried. "The Chief is the Werewolf!"

"So you figured it out!" he roared as he leaped and blocked the door. "Nice detective work." Then he flashed his claws! "Not that it'll do you any good!"

"Maybe not," said Sam. "But I think this will."

Sam held up his walkie-talkie, showing the Chief it had been on the whole time. The rest of the police department must have heard everything!

Sam had already known the Chief was the Werewolf. Figures. We were related, after all.

 "**RRRRRRR!**" the Chief roared angrily.
He leaped across his desk and swung a huge claw
right at my chest.

Just as it was about to hit . . .
RRRRRRRUMMBLE! The room shook!

It was another earthquake!

It only lasted a second, but that was long enough
to throw off the Chief's swing!

And that's when the police burst in with their guns
drawn! The Chief put his clawed hands up.

Sam rushed over to where I had fallen on the
ground. The Chief's claws had missed my chest, but
they'd still hit something vital.

My journal! I'd lost a few pages. But better them
than me!

It took a dozen policemen to drag the Chief away.
Even more showed up to slap Sam on the back.
He was a hero!

They all told Sam they had had hunches that the Chief was no good. But it was Sam who had finally proven that to be true.

Sam left with them to take my journal (which was now evidence) to be processed. I spent a few minutes waiting in the Chief's empty office.

Pretty quickly, a police officer came and handed me my journal. He slapped me on my back (I guess back-slapping is something police officers like to do?) and thanked me for helping Sam discover that the Chief was the Werewolf. He assured me I was no longer a suspect and that I was free to go.

I wanted to say goodbye to Sam. But the officer made it clear Sam was busy making sure the Chief stayed behind bars for good and that I should get going.

So I left police HQ. As I did, something fell out of my journal.

It was a note. From Sam!

J.D. —

  Sorry for the bum's rush, but I had to get you out of there
quick. If you had stayed, you would have had to make a
statement and stick around to testify against the Chief. And
I know you don't have time for that. You've got to shake a leg
and find the rest of your cousins.

  Your cousins are lucky to have you on the case. It took me
until now to finally solve a mystery worthy of Samuel Hammer.
You did it on the first try! But I guess I shouldn't be
surprised. Because you've got the same detective's eye as
my grandfather.

  As soon as I make sure the Chief is locked up in the big
house for good, I'll come and help you. In the meantime, I put
something else in your journal to keep you busy.

  Your cousin,
  Sam

I saw that Sam had stuffed something else in my journal. The pages from my dad's police file!

There were probably a ton of clues in there that would lead me to the rest of my cousins!

I was psyched. If this had been the end of my story, it totally would have been a happy ending.

But that's not the way life works.

It keeps going and going. If you're lucky.

I had a lot of cousins out there who might not be so lucky. Unless I figured out where the rest of my dad's body parts came from. Fast!

And that was just what I was going to do!

THE END?

NOT AS SCARY AS HE LOOKS!

Scott Sonneborn has written dozens of books, one circus (for Ringling Bros. and Barnum & Bailey), and a bunch of TV shows. He's been nominated for one Emmy and spent three very cool years working at DC Comics. He lives in Los Angeles with his wife and their two sons.

COOLEST ILLUSTRATOR EVER!

Timothy Banks is an award-winning illustrator known for his ability to create magically quirky illustrations for kids and adults. He has a Master of Fine Arts degree in Illustration from the Savannah College of Art & Design, and he also teaches fledgling art students in his spare time. Timothy lives in Charleston, SC, with his wonderful wife, two beautiful daughters, and two crazy pugs.

I, J.D., dedicate this journal to my dad,
FRANKENSTEIN'S MONSTER.

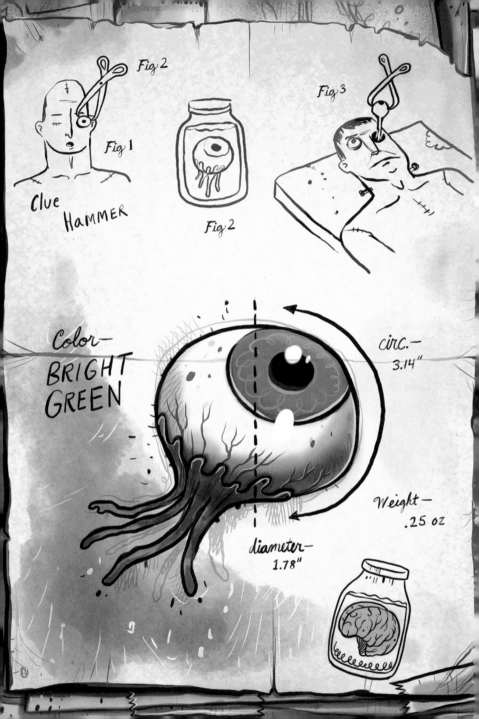